Inside
Mary Elizabeth's House

For Julie Watts

PUFFIN BOOKS

Published by the Penguin Group
Penguin Group (Australia)
250 Camberwell Road
Camberwell, Victoria 3124, Australia
(a division of Pearson Australia Group Pty Ltd)
Penguin Group (USA) Inc.
375 Hudson Street, New York, New York 10014, USA
Penguin Group (Canada)
10 Alcorn Avenue, Toronto, Ontario, Canada M4V 3B2
(a division of Pearson Penguin Canada Inc.)
Penguin Books Ltd
80 Strand, London WC2R 0RL, England
Penguin Ireland
25 St Stephen's Green, Dublin 2, Ireland
(a division of Penguin Books Ltd)
Penguin Books India Pvt Ltd
11, Community Centre, Panchsheel Park, New Delhi-110 017, India
Penguin Group (NZ)
Cnr Airborne and Rosedale Roads, Albany, Auckland, New Zealand
(a division of Pearson New Zealand Ltd)
Penguin Books (South Africa) (Pty) Ltd
24 Sturdee Avenue, Rosebank, Johannesburg 2196, South Africa

Penguin Books Ltd, Registered Offices: 80 Strand, London WC2R 0RL,
England

First published by Penguin Books Australia, 2000
Published in Puffin Books, 2001

7 9 10 8 6

Copyright © Pamela Allen, 2000

Designed by Deborah Brash/Brash Design Pty Ltd, Sydney
Typeset in 24pt Stone Serif by Brash Design Pty Ltd
Printed in Australia through the Australian Book Connection.

National Library of Australia
Cataloguing-in-Publication data:

Allen, Pamela
Inside Mary Elizabeth's house.

ISBN 0 140 56711 9.

I. Title.

A823.3

www.puffin.com.au

Inside
Mary Elizabeth's House

Pamela Allen

Puffin Books

Here is Mary Elizabeth's house.

This is Mary Elizabeth,

and these are the boys.

On Monday morning,
on the way to school,
Mary Elizabeth
said to the boys,

'There's a monster at my house.'

'We don't believe you!' they said.

'They don't believe me,' she said.

On Tuesday morning
Mary Elizabeth said to the boys,
'There's a monster at my house
with red blood-shot eyes
and sharp pointy teeth.

He's rough and he's rowdy
and he jumps on my bed.'

'We *don't* believe you,' they said.

'They *won't* believe me,' she said.

'Huh! Huh! Ugh!'

On Wednesday morning
Mary Elizabeth said to the boys,
'There's a monster at my house
with red blood-shot eyes
and sharp pointy teeth.

He's rough and he's rowdy
and jumps on my bed.
He doesn't wash and
he won't clean his teeth.

My mother says that he'll have to go
but he likes it at my house,
he told me so.'

'We don't BELIEVE you!' they cried.
And they laughed.

'They STILL won't believe me,' she said.

'Huh! Huh! Ugh! Huh! Ugh! Ugh!'

On Thursday morning
on the way to school,
Mary Elizabeth said to the boys,
'There IS a monster at my house.'

'We don't believe you,
we don't believe you,
we don't believe you,'
they chanted.

Mary Elizabeth smiled.

'I'll show you,' she said.

'Come for dinner tonight at seven.'

'Yum! FOOD!' the boys shouted.

'It's the house painted red.

Number eleven.

You'll see,' said Mary Elizabeth.

Later that night,
about a quarter to seven,
the boys set out for number eleven.

'She did say number eleven, didn't she?'

Knock! Knock! Knock!

It was seven o'clock.

Mary Elizabeth came to the door.

'We're here and we're hungry,' the boys cried.
'What's for dinner?'
 Slowly Mary Elizabeth smiled her sweet smile.
'Come in,' she said, 'and see . . .'

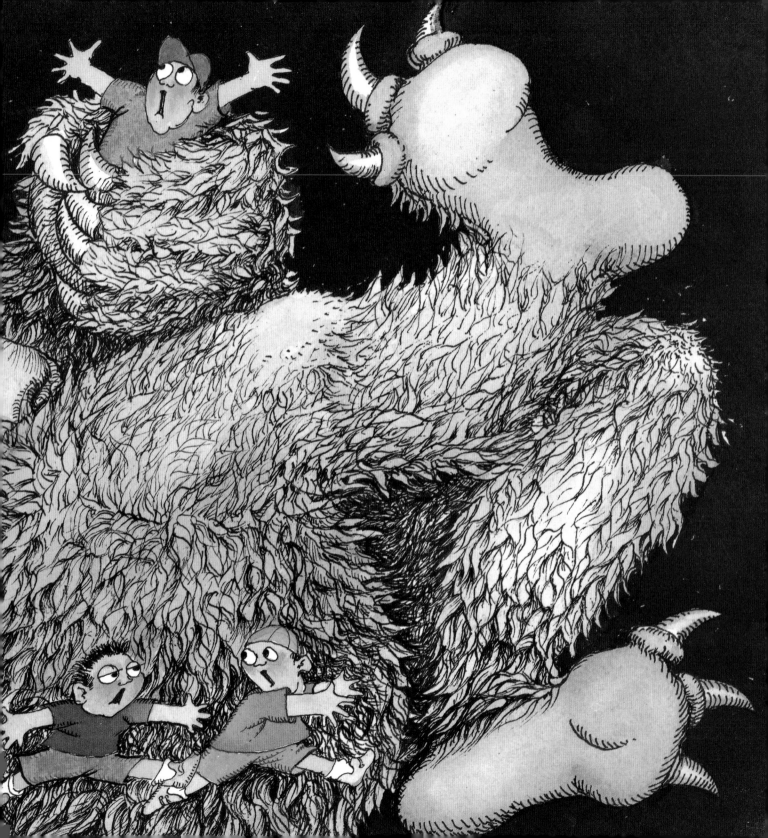

'YAAAAAAAAAAAA

AAAAHHHHH!'

'Now they believe me,' she said.